SAKE JOCK

FANTAGRAPHICS BOOKS

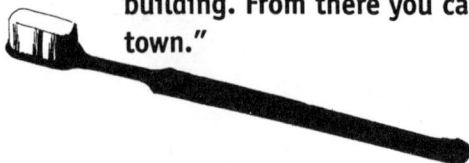

Sake Jock is published by Fantagraphics Books, and is copyright ©1995 Fantagraphics Books. All characters, stories, and art ©1995 Serinido/Garo, Imiri Sakabashira. No part of this book may be reproduced without written permission from Fantagraphics Books, Serinido/Garo and Imiri Sakabashira. No similarity between any of the names, characters, persons, and institutions in *Sake Jock* and those of any living or dead person is intended, and any such similarity that may exist is purely coincidental. First printing: October, 1995. Available from the publisher for $11.00 postpaid. Fantagraphics Books,7563 Lake City Way NE, Seattle, WA 98115. Printed in Canada.

P.13   WHAT A MIXED UP WORLD!

Yasuji Tanioka was one of the most popular cartoonists of the '70s and '80s, inventing several popular catch phrases still in use today. Now in its 27th year, the Tanioka Yasuji award is considered a gateway to a successful cartoonist's career.

p.33   MILLION DOLLARS

Although he was born on the northern island of Hokkaido, Yoshiharu Mitsumoto's heart belongs to the suburbs of America. He spends his spare time following the careers of wrestlers such as Jimmy Snuka and the music of the Kinks and Van Morrison. His first feature-length book will be released this year in Japan.

p.55   KISSES • KIRIKO NANANAN

Naoki and Shunichi Karasawa are a team popular with many *Otaku* (die-hard fans) for their autobiographical stories. Naoki currently produces over 30 stories a month, published everywhere from the underground to children's magazines.

head honcho: ADAM GLICKMAN
co-translator: MARI TAMURA
editorial supervisor: GARY GROTH
cover design and production/design assistance: JEREMY EATON
cover color: JEFF JOHNSON
publishers: GARY GROTH
AND KIM THOMPSON

Thanks to Yukiko Oyama, who worked harder to make this book happen than anyone else. You're the coolest!

INTRODUCTION

The content of most comics the world over has never much differed from their American counterparts in subject matter if not in style: super heroes or their equivalent, sophomoric genre-bound stories. We all know that comics have always been pretty much a boys' club, and most young men (no matter where they're from) want to read about flying robots and teenage kung fu sex queens. This kind of stuff is crammed down our throats at an early age, and while the ingredients differ from place to place, it all tastes suspiciously like fast food to me.

In Japan it sometimes seems as if the overriding consideration to a cartoonist is that the length of time it takes to read a story not exceed the average Tokyo commute, and it's hard to condemn these aspiring young artists for conforming to this commercial requirement; after all, a successful strip can earn television appearances, animated feature films, celebrity, and most importantly, a lotta yen.

Unfortunately, most of the artists featured here are living quite a different lifestyle. They've endured long hours and low-rent apartments in order to create their own personal visions. For the past 30 years a monthly magazine called *Garo* has been the main showcase for Japanese cartoonists who won't (or can't) prostitute their talent. It's a great that such a magazine exists in Japan, but most American comics readers know nothing of Japanese alternative comics. Alternative comics artists and their publishers throughout the world need to help each other gain a wider audience because we're all in the same boat, broke and underappreciated. This collection of underground Japanese comics is an attempt to shrink the global village a little and introduce the West to the growing Japanese alternative comics scene few of us even knew existed.

As we head toward the 21st century other cultures become more accessible to us and while you probably wouldn't want to travel to Japan to meet this oddball crew, you should find it fun spending the afternoon with them in the comfort of your own living room.

Adam Glickman,
Editor

马马虎虎

HORSE　HORSE　TIGER　TIGER

逆柱 SAKABASHIRA IMIRI いみり

GO DOWN TO CHINA TOWN AND GET ME SOME HOMEOPATHIC MEDICINE!

YEAH... O.K.

THAT HUGE FISH IS ONLY $1.78! THAT'S DAMN CHEAP!

IT KINDA SMELLS LIKE SHIT!

PROBABLY ROTTEN.

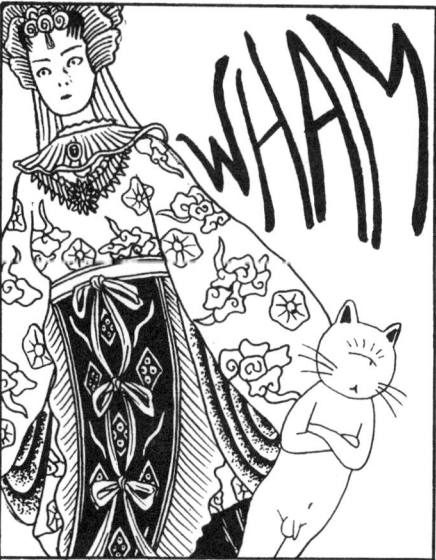

WHAM

WHAT THE HELL?

YEAH, IT'S JUST SKIN AND INNARDS.

9

GIMME THAT BLACK GOAT'S HEAD.

PRETTY HARD HEADED!

IT SURE DOESNT TASTE SO HOT

WHAT A MIXED UP WORLD!

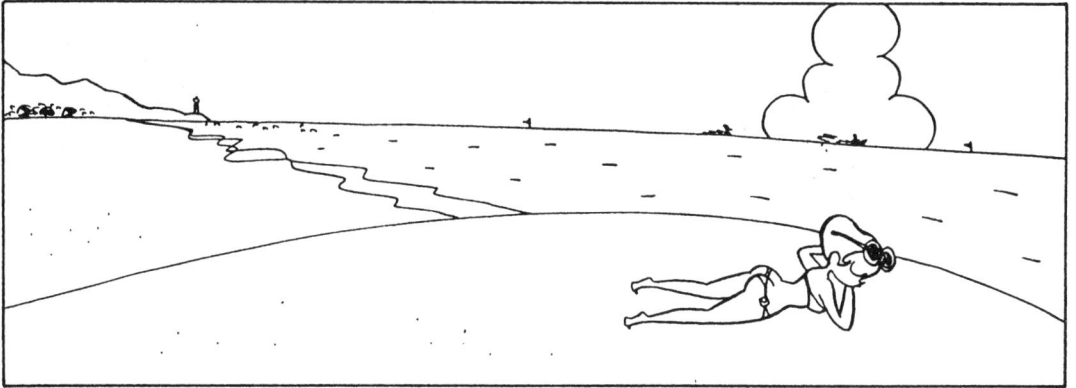

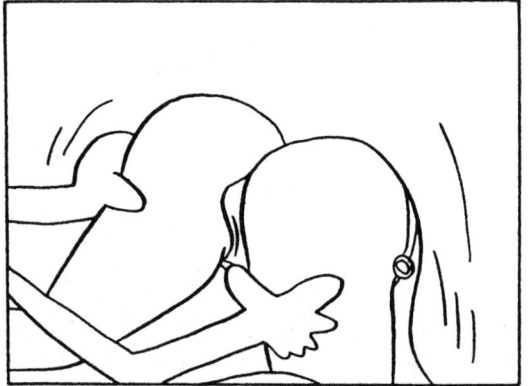

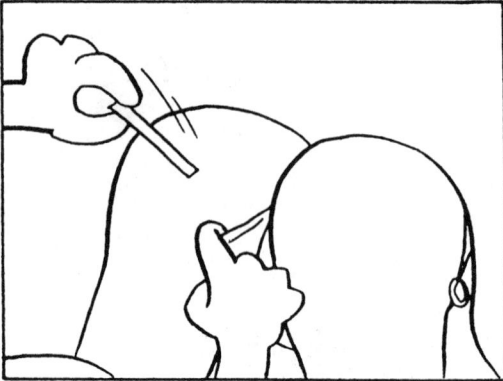

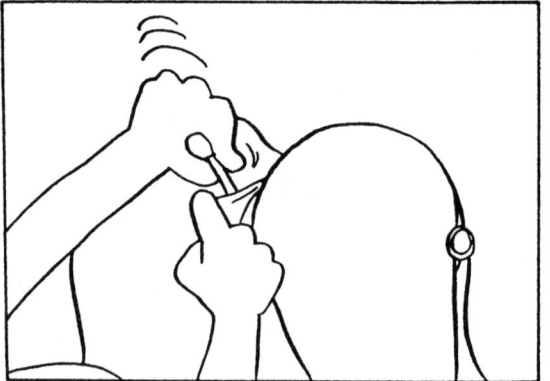

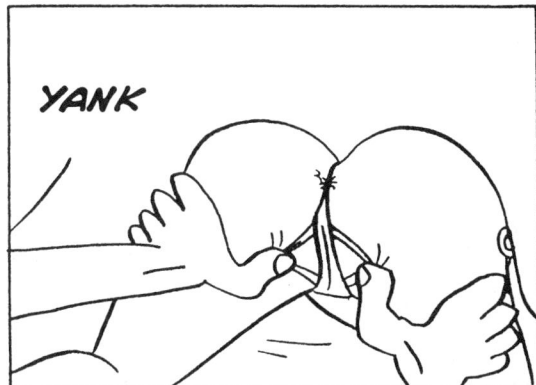

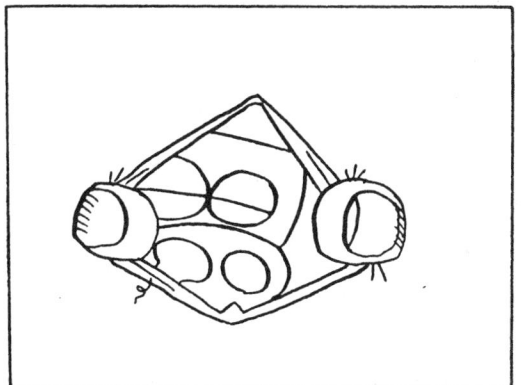

16

WHAT A MIXED UP WORLD!

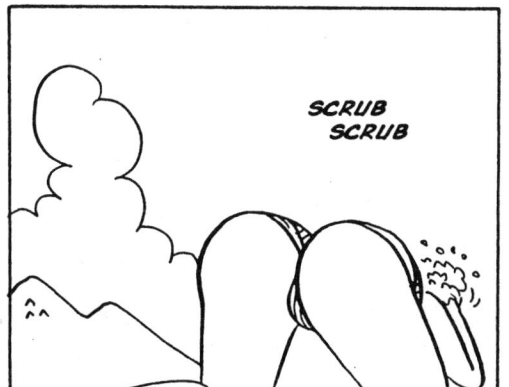

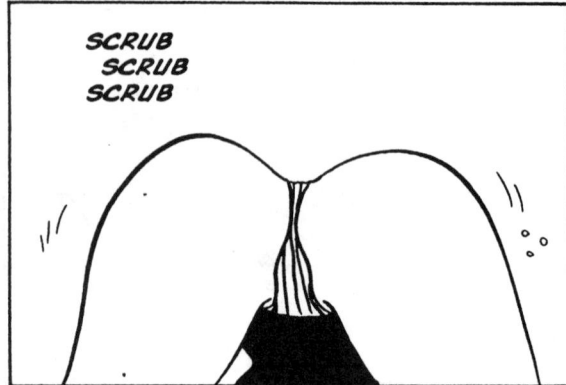

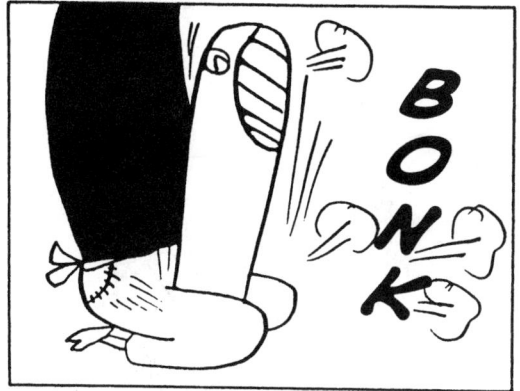

WHAT A MIXED UP WORLD!

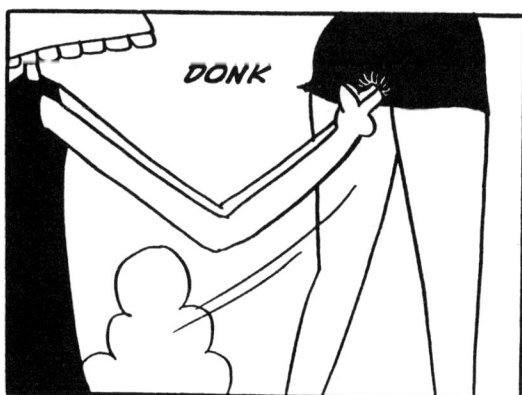

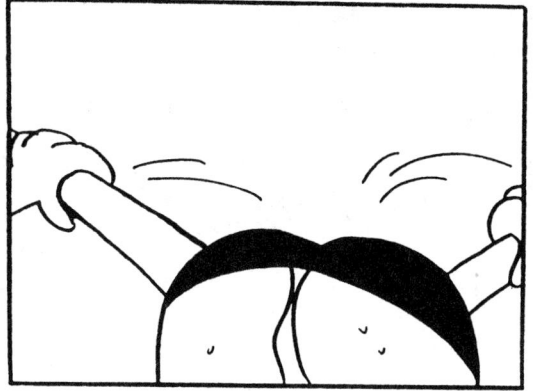

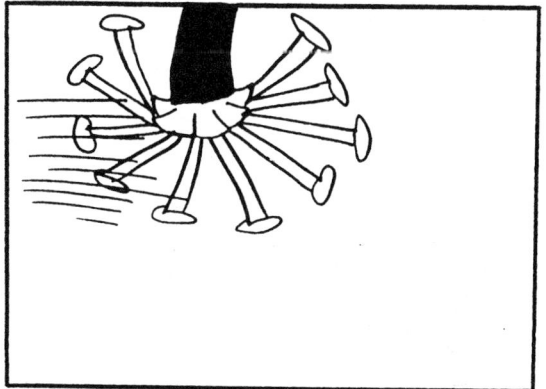

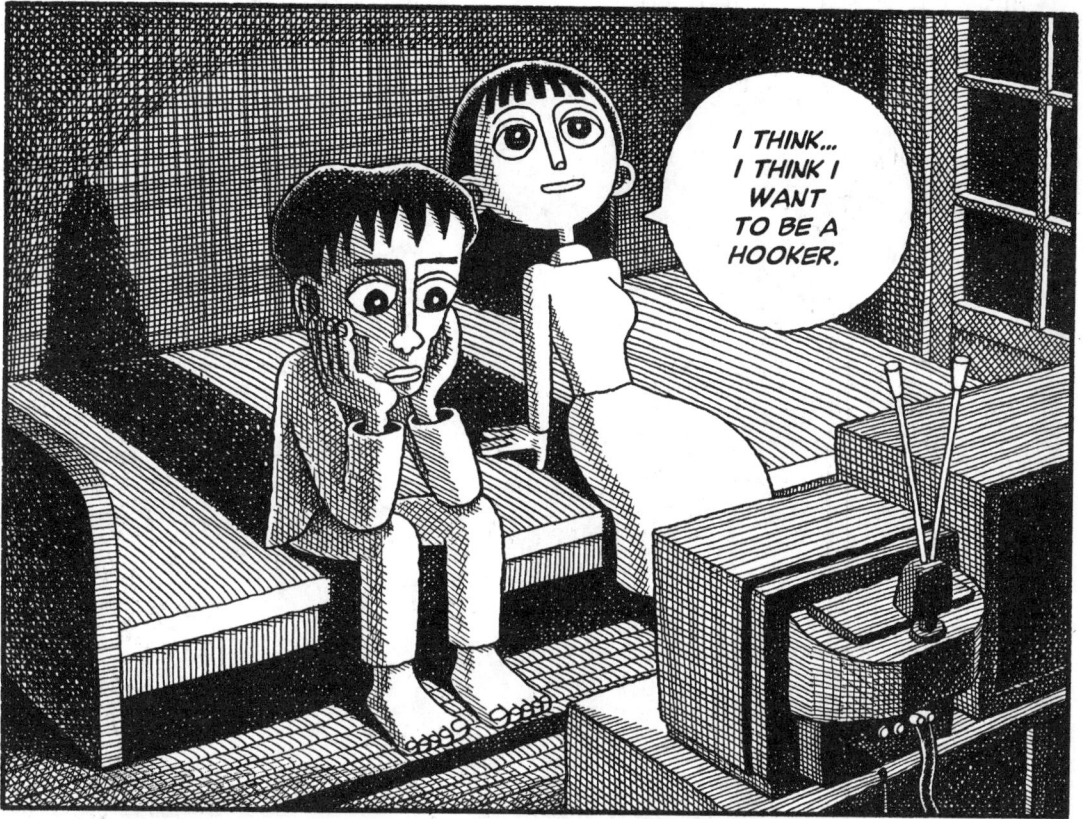

A HOOKER'S ROOM

HOLD UP!

I DON'T LIKE THE WAY YOU UNDRESS.

WHA?

YOU'RE NOT SUPPOSED TO TAKE OFF YOUR PANTS FIRST.

YOU TAKE OFF YOUR SHIRT FIRST.

MM... O.K.

IF YOU INSIST.

HEY, MAYBE I DON'T LIKE THE WAY YOU UNDRESS EITHER.

The Proper Way To Undress

I'M RIGHT. DON'T ASK ME WHY.

WELL...

I GUESS MAYBE YOU ARE.

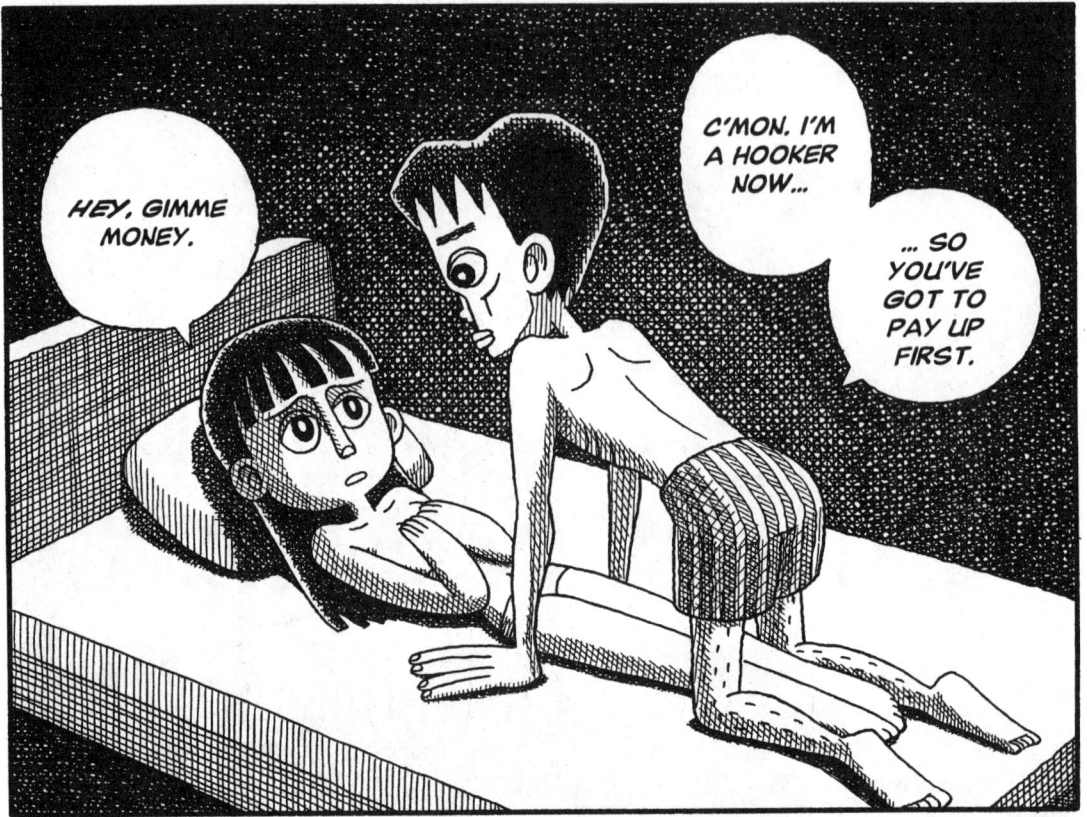

SO YOU'RE A HOOKER NOW. WHAT EXACTLY DOES THAT ENTAIL?

NUTHIN MUCH...

... I JUST WANTED TO USE THAT WORD.

OH YEAH?

THAT BRAIN OF YOURS IS ALWAYS WORKING, HUH?

YEP. ALWAYS WORKING.

HEY! LET'S EAT!

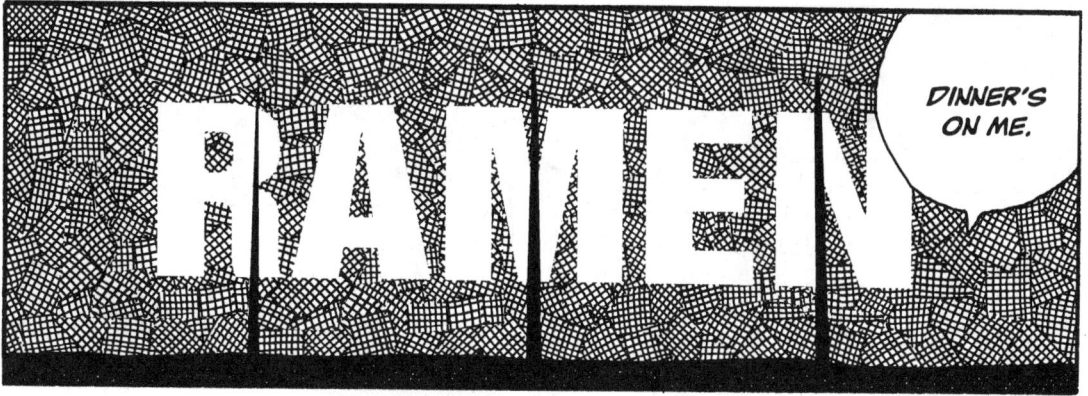

31

THEN I WANT TO BE ...

... YOUR PIMP.

....!

O.K!

THAT'S A GREAT IDEA!

HA HA HA... A HOOKER AND HER PIMP.

WHAT A PAIR!

WE'RE GONNA MAKE A GREAT TEAM.

IT'LL BE FUN!

YOU WANT ANOTHER DUMPLING?

RAMEN

YEAH, O.K.

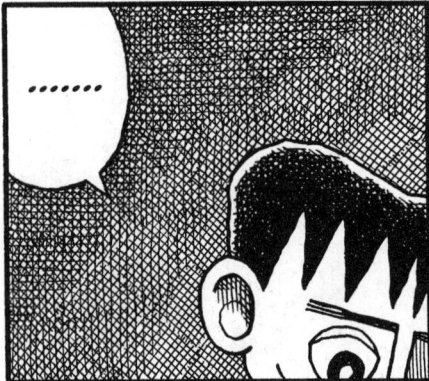

....

32

WOO! YEAH! WOO!

... AND NOW TO INTRODUCE THE "GREAT, ROMANESQUE, WILD, BORNEO INTERNATIONAL FILM FESTIVAL" GRAND PRIX WINNER.

DIRECTOR, HOW DO YOU FEEL ABOUT RECEIVING THIS GREAT HONOR?

HMM... LET'S SEE...

I'D LIKE MY AUDIENCE TO APPRECIATE THAT THIS PIECE DREW INSPIRATION FROM A DRASTICALLY DIFFERENT PLANE THAN THE AVERAGE FILM. THE RESTORATION OF AN ANTIQUE BEAUTY THROUGH THE EMPHASIS OF SILENCE AND RESTRAINT.

A TRUE ESTABLISHMENT OF JAPANESE IDENTITY THROUGHOUT THE FILM MAY OR MAY NOT BE INTERPRETED AS SARCASM, OR THE ANTITHESIS OF THE FUSION RATIONALIZED BY MODERN WESTERN DOCTRINE. ... OR SOMETHING LIKE THAT.

I SEE...

BY MAKING THIS FILM, I PAY HOMAGE, TO THE GREAT DIRECTOR YASUJIROU OZU.

... OOOH

ONE FINAL QUESTION. WHAT DOES THE WORD "FILM" MEAN TO YOU?

HMM-MM...

LOVE

THANK YOU VERY MUCH. NOW, PLEASE SIT BACK AND ENJOY THIS WONDERFUL PIECE OF WORK.

YEAH YO O W WOO

Million
Dollars

IT'S TOO LOW!

NEXT, PLEASE...

THANKS SO MUCH FOR YOUR PATRONAGE. OOOH! BEAN SPROUTS!

DON'T FORGET, WE ALWAYS APPRECIATE YOUR BUSINESS. YUM! PLANTERS PEANUTS... SUGAR SMACKS...

YOUR TOTAL IS...

RING

EIGHTEEN EIGHTY, PLEASE.

... AND 120 MILLION DOLLARS IS YOUR CHANGE.

....

....

HA HA HA

STOP IT!

HEH

PLEASE EXCUSE MY FATHER. THANK YOU VERY MUCH.

GOOD BYE

O.K. DAD, I'LL WORK THE REGISTER NOW.

BUT THAT'S MY JOB.

HELLO.

WHY HELLO, MRS. SASAKI.

YOU ALL MUST BE SO TIRED, STAYING OPEN SO LATE AND ALL...

OH, VERY MUCH SO. BUT WE REALLY HAVE NO CHOICE, SINCE WE GET SO MUCH LATE NIGHT BUSINESS.

BY THE WAY, I'M SO SORRY ABOUT THE REPUTATION YOUR STORE HAS RECEIVED...

... DUE TO YOUR FATHER'S ANTICS.

IT APPEARS HE'S GROWN SENILE.

YES, I QUITE AGREE.

NOT THAT I CARE SO MUCH, BUT THE OTHER DAY HE GAVE ME SLIGHTLY LESS THAN THE CORRECT AMOUNT OF CHANGE. IT'S UNIMPORTANT TO ME...

... BUT I WORRY ABOUT YOUR OTHER CUSTOMERS. ... OH, YOU DON'T HAVE TO...

I'M SO SORRY.

IT'S SUCH A SHAME. HE CAN'T EVEN RECOGNIZE HIS OWN SENILITY.

IT SADDENS MY HEART TO WATCH SUCH A WELL-SPOKEN, PRODUCTIVE MAN DECLINE LIKE THAT.

HE WAS ONCE SO THRIFTY AND AMBITIOUS. HE BEGAN AS JUST A LOWLY STREET VENDOR, BUT WORKED HARD AND CONTINUED TO EXPAND. AT ONE TIME, HE EVEN HAD HOPES OF OPENING A CHAIN OF STORES.

BUT HE JUST HASN'T GOT IT ANY MORE.

OH, NO. HE'S STILL YOUNG YET...

NOPE. HE'S NO GOOD. N-O-O GOOOD.

HE'S SO ADAMANT ABOUT WORKING AT THE REGISTER.

SOON, I'LL JUST HAVE TO MAKE IT CLEAR THAT HE'S NO LONGER CAPABLE OF HANDLING THE RESPONSIBILITY.

YES, I UNDERSTAND.

GOOD NIGHT.

YOU'RE NOT BUYING ANYTHING?

O.K.

I'LL BE OUT FOR A BIT.

OH NO. I TRIED MY BEST TO KEEP UP WITH YOU GUYS...

... BUT I ADMIT THAT SOMETIMES I CAN BE A LITTLE SLOW.

A BIT?

EH

STOP IT.

I'LL GO TAKE MY NAP NOW.

WOULD YOU LIKE YOUR DINNER FIRST, DAD?

NO THANKS. I'VE EATEN.

NO YOU HAVEN'T.

TOSHIKO. HAVE YOU SEEN MY OIL OF OLAY?

MY OIL OF OLAY'S NOT HERE.

DIDN'T ONE WORD OF THAT GET THROUGH TO YOU?

HERE! USE A BAR OF SOAP!

WHAM

SOAP

J...JEEZUS, TOSHIKO. WAS THAT REALLY NECESSARY?

THE FARMER IN THE DELL, THE FARMER IN THE DELL...

HI-HO

THE MERRY-O...

GRANDPA'S ROOM

SLIDE

HI HO MHH HMM !

AHH...

39

... NO MORE "MILLION DOLLAR" WISE CRACKS...

HEY, DAD. ARE YOU GOING OUT TONIGHT?

YEP! I'VE BEEN INVITED TO A REUNION WITH A BUNCH OF MY OLD ARMY BUDDIES. I PROBABLY WONT BE HOME TONIGHT, SO COULD YOU WATCH THE SHOP?

NO... I GUESS I DON'T NEED TO WORRY ABOUT THAT. DO I?

DAD...

... IT REALLY TEARS ME UP INSIDE...

... THAT I CAN'T DO MORE TO HELP YOU WHEN YOU'RE FEELING DOWN.

SNIF SNIF

NO SON, YOU DON'T HAVE TO WORRY ABOUT ME.

THERE SHOULD NEVER BE HARD FEELINGS AMONG FAMILY

YOU KNOW... IT'S FUNNY HOW YOU CARE SO MUCH FOR ME...

... AND WE'RE NOT EVEN RELATED BY BLOOD.

SNIFFLE

CRAAAP

I'VE BEEN SO LUCKY TO HAVE A SON-IN-LAW LIKE YOU.

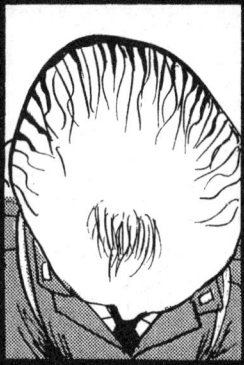

DONG

THE AUTOPSY REPORT SHOWED THAT HIS BRAIN HAD BEEN HEMORRHAGING FROM THE PREVIOUS DAY.

WHEN YOU HIT HIM WITH THAT SOAP...

NO ONE CARES. HE WAS SO OLD EVERYONE'LL FIGURE HE KILLED HIMSELF FROM DRINKING.

SHHH

EVEN NOW, HE'S STILL A PAIN IN MY ASS. THIS FUNERAL'S GONNA COST A FORTUNE!

DONG

BUT WHEN YOU...

GOOD EVENING!

GOOD EVENING, MRS. SASAKI.

I'M SO SORRY TO HEAR ABOUT YOUR FATHER. HE PASSED ALONG SO SUDDENLY.

WELL, HE HAD BEEN SO STEADFAST ALL HIS LIFE.

... BUT NOW THAT HE'S GONE, I FEEL AS IF MAYBE I SHOULD HAVE BEEN MORE LENIENT ABOUT HIS "MILLION DOLLAR" GAMES...

THE

ABALONE

CAT

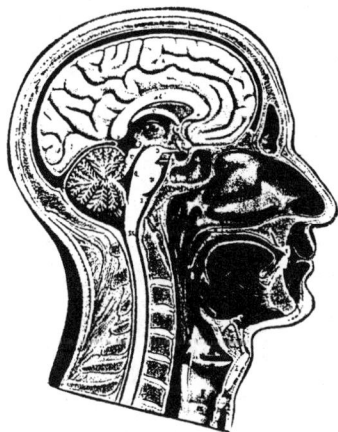

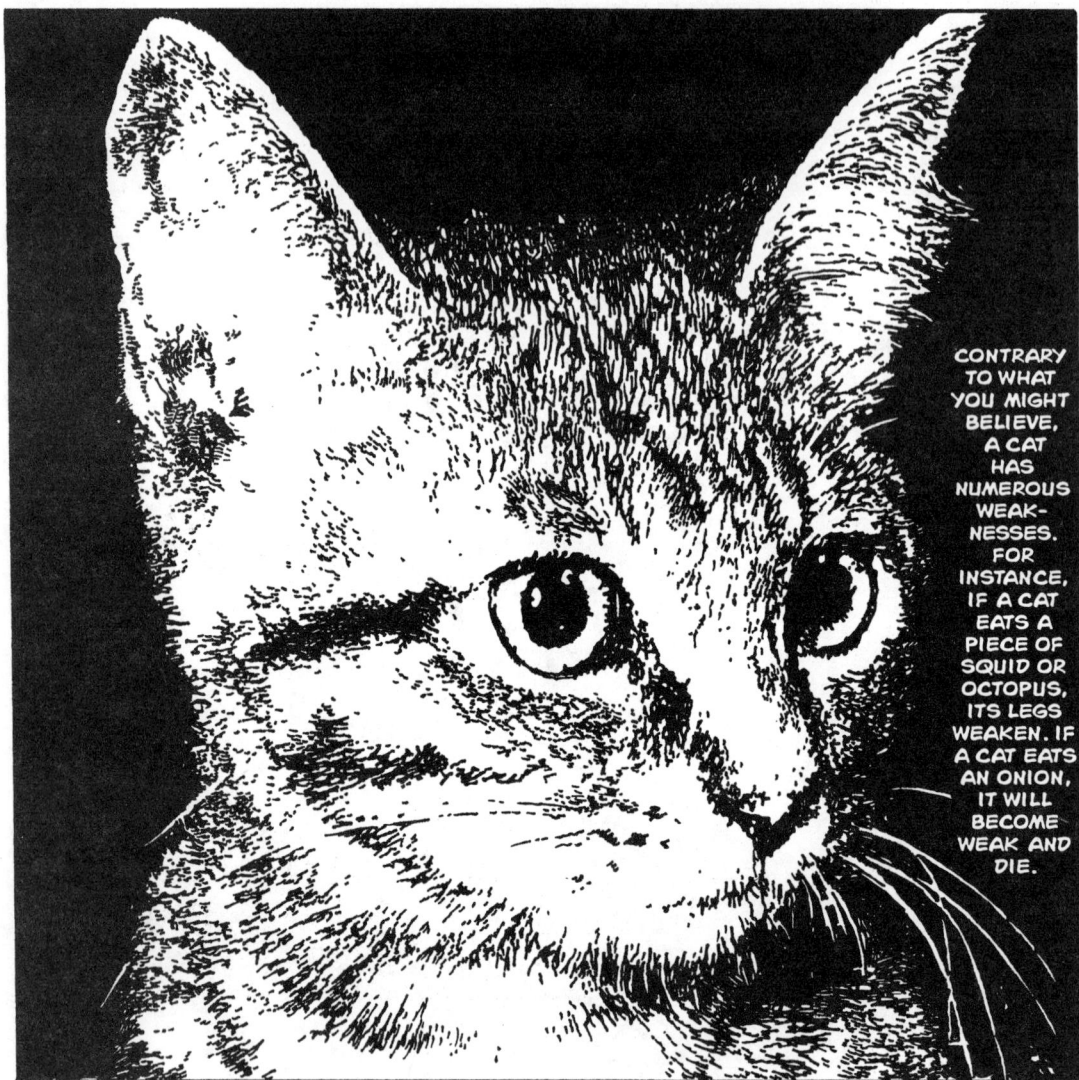

CONTRARY TO WHAT YOU MIGHT BELIEVE, A CAT HAS NUMEROUS WEAKNESSES. FOR INSTANCE, IF A CAT EATS A PIECE OF SQUID OR OCTOPUS, ITS LEGS WEAKEN. IF A CAT EATS AN ONION, IT WILL BECOME WEAK AND DIE.

AN ANCIENT TEACHING STATES THAT YOU MUSN'T FEED THEM ABALONE. OTERWISE THE CAT'S EARS WILL ROT AND FALL OFF.

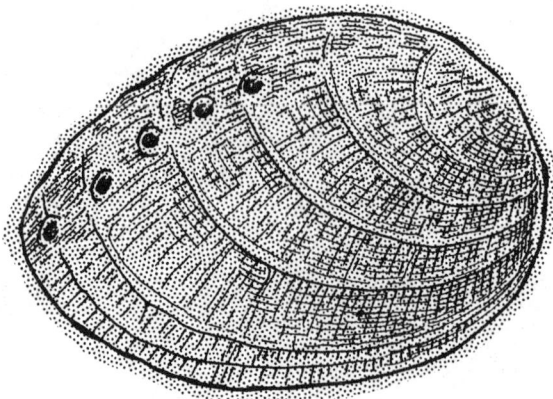

YOU'RE PROBABLY ALSO WONDERING WHY THE CAT'S EARS WOULD FALL OFF, YET IT WOULDN'T DIE.

"WHO'D FEED A CAT EXPENSIVE ABALONE, ANYWAY? " YOU ASK?

LET ME EXPLAIN. THE PROBLEM BEGINS IN THE ABALONE'S LIVER. THAT IS, THE LIVER STORES CHLOROPHYLL FROM THE SEAWEED IT EATS. THE CAT'S STOMACH LACKS THE ENZYME REQUIRED TO BREAK DOWN THIS CHLOROPHYLL, AND THEREFORE IT'S ABSORBED BY ITS BLOOD VESSELS.

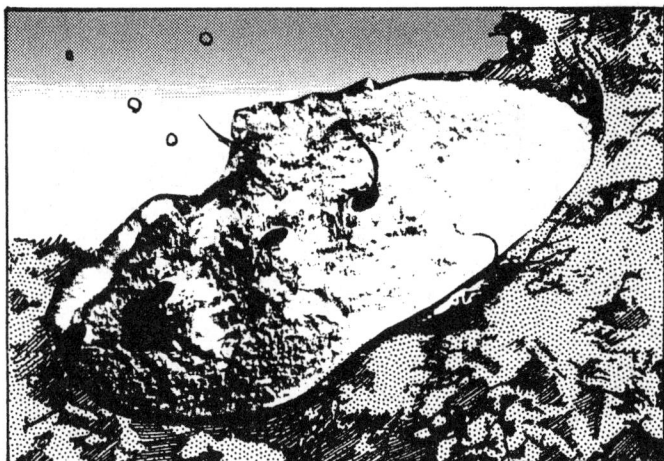

AS A RESULT, THESE THIN BLOOD VESSELS ARE UNABLE TO PROVIDE EACH CELL WITH THE PROPER AMOUNT OF OXYGEN, AND THEREFORE THE EARS FALL OFF.

A CAT'S EARS ARE SO THIN THAT THE BLOOD VESSELS ARE VISIBLE THROUGH THE SKIN'S LINING. WHEN THE CHLOROPHYLL REACHES A BLOOD VESSEL, PHOTOSYNTHESIS OCCURS, AND THE CHLOROPHYLL BEGINS TO REPRODUCE ITSELF.

... AND THAT'S HOW WE GET THE ABALONE CAT.

AN OLD COLLEGE BUDDY OF MINE USED TO WORK AT THE TSUKIJI MARKET. ONCE HE CAME ACROSS A BUNCH OF ABALONE CATS LIVING IN THE WAREHOUSE. BOY, WAS HE SURPRISED!

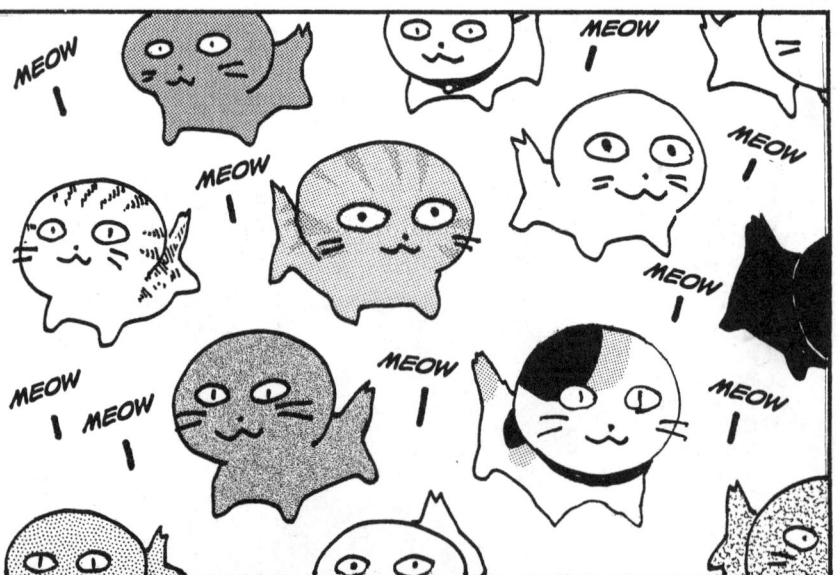

MEOW
MEOW
MEOW
MEOW
MEOW
MEOW
MEOW
MEOW
MEOW

I HAD ANOTHER FRIEND WHO HIT HIS HEAD IN A CAR WRECK, AND HAD TO BE EXAMINED BY A CAT SCAN.

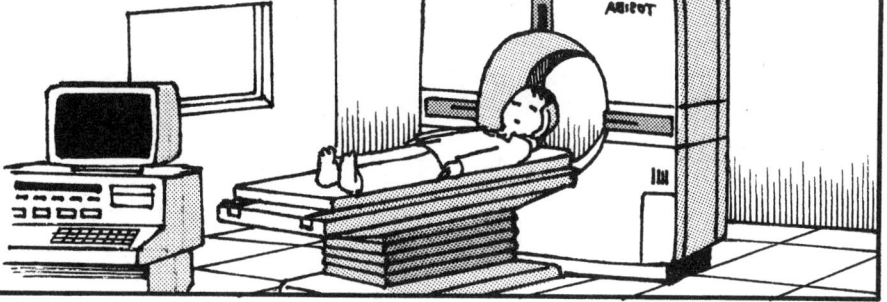

I GOT PRETTY SCARED GOING UNDER THAT BIG ARCH. MAYBE THEY'D TURN UP THE ELECTRICITY TOO HIGH AND SLICE ME IN TWO OR SOMETHING...

IN THE OLD DAYS, THEY DIDN'T HAVE ANYTHING LIKE CAT SCANS, THE ONLY WAY TO EXAMINE A SECTION OF THE BODY WAS TO ACTUALLY CUT IT OPEN!

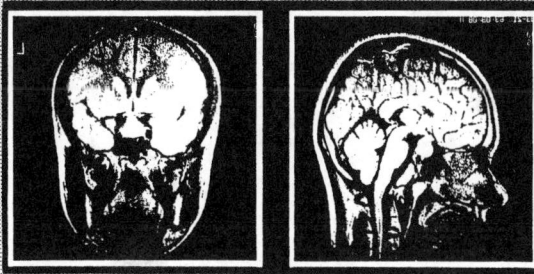

COLLEGE PROFESSORS, AND PEOPLE LIKE THAT, WOULD CREATE SAMPLES BY SAWING OFF BODY PARTS!

OHGAI MORI, THE FAMOUS AUTHOR, HAD A SON WHO ONCE WROTE AN INTERESTING STORY ABOUT TAKING A SAMPLE FROM THE BRAIN'S FRONTAL LOBE.

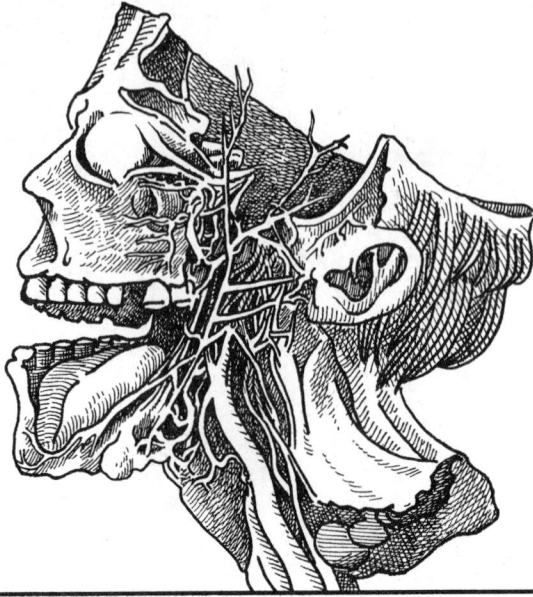

BUT IN THE 20'S, TOKYO UNIVERSITY HOSPITAL DIDN'T POSSESS A FRIDGE LARGE ENOUGH TO FREEZE AN ENTIRE BODY ...

"... OF COURSE THE BODY MUST BE COMPLETELY FROZEN IN ORDER TO REMOVE A PROPER SAMPLE..."

... SO THEY'D TAKE THE BODIES OUTSIDE IN THE MIDDLE OF WINTER AND COVER THEM IN SALT WATER.

THEN LEAVE THE BODY OUTSIDE UNTIL IT WAS FROZEN, AT WHICH POINT, THEY'D SIMPLY CUT IT UP.

50

MY UNCLE TOLD THE CAB DRIVER GRANDPA WAS REALLY SICK, AND HE DIDN'T EVEN CHARGE HIM FOR THE RIDE!

ARE YOU O.K.?

CAN YOU HOLD IT A BIT LONGER?

WE'RE ALMOST THERE!

AFTERWARDS, GRANDPA'S COFFIN WOULDN'T FIT INTO OUR APARTMENT BUILDING'S ELEVATOR.

SO HE HAD TO BE PIGGY-BACKED TO HIS OWN FUNREAL.

HERE'S ANOTHER STORY. MY FRIEND'S DAD WAS A NEWSPAPER REPORTER.

aaaah

ONE DAY, HE WAS IN A HELICOPTER COVERING A STORY, WHEN HE LEANED OUT TO GET A BETTER VIEW, AND FELL TO HIS DEATH.

click

THE CAMERA MAN QUICKLY LEAPED UP AND TOOK A PICTURE.

THE LAST PICTURE OF HIS DAD'S LIFE LOOKED LIKE THIS...

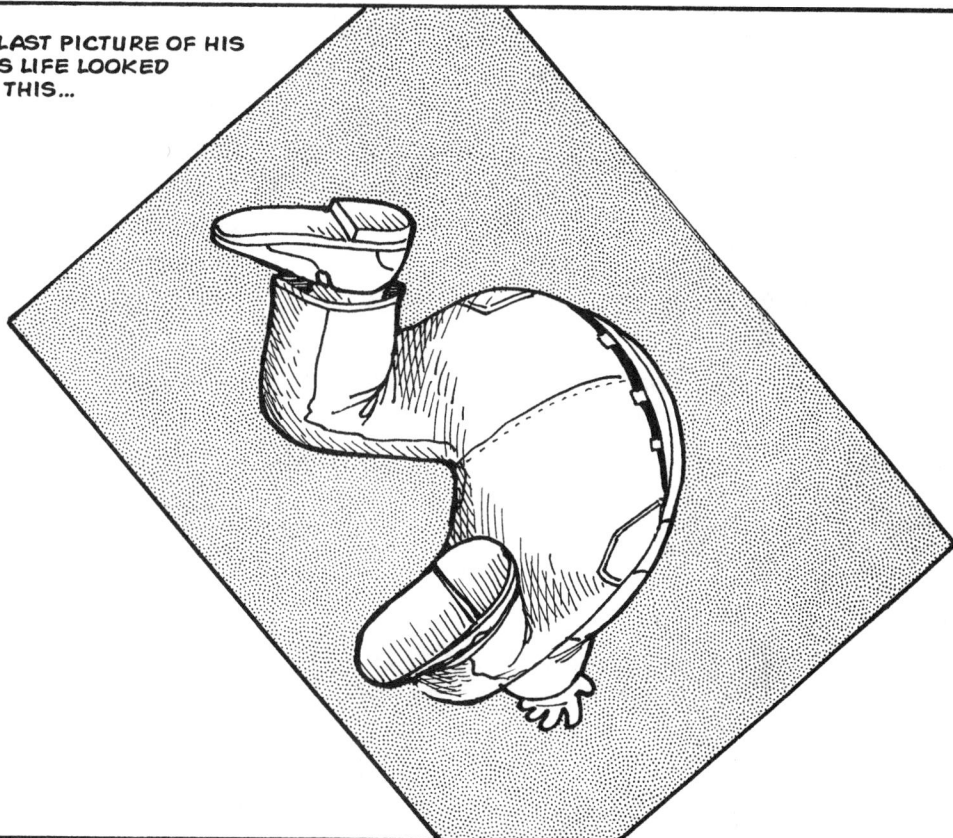

AT THE MOMENT I'M SITTING IN A SHINJUKU COFEE SHOP, AND I'M TRYING TO FINISH THIS STORY, BUT THE PEOPLE BEHIND ME ARE REALLY DISTRACTING.

"...YOU KNOW THAT WAS SUCH A LONG MOVIE."

"...YEAH, THE MAIN CHARACTER... AH, WHAT'S HIS NAME... AH, YEAH! HESTON... CHARLES HESTON! HE PLAYED CHRIST. NO, WAIT, IT WASN'T CHRIST. MOSES, THAT'S IT! HOW COULD I FORGET THAT? SO HE LEADS HIS PEOPLE OUT OF EYGPT. WAIT... WAS IT EYGPT? THERE WERE PYRAMIDS SO IT MUST'VE BEEN EYGPT. BUT IT COULDN'T HAVE BEEN ABOUT JESUS BECAUSE THE MOVIE TOOK PLACE BEFORE CHRISTIANITY. YEAH, THAT WAS STUPID. ...SO THIS PART'S GREAT! THE KING COMES, AND ALL THE EYGPTIANS GO *"YEEAH!"* AND THE SEA DIVIDES IN TWO RIGHT DOWN THE MIDDLE. *HA! HA! WHAT? THE NAME OF THE SEA? I DON'T KNOW. ...WAIT! IT WAS THE MEDITERRANEAN!*

THE ABALONE CAT

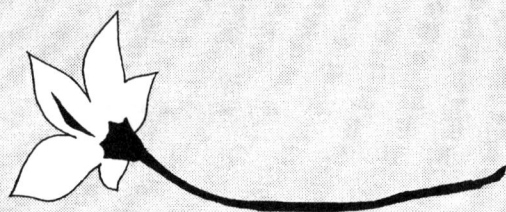

KISSES • KIRIKO NANANAN

A HA HA HA HA

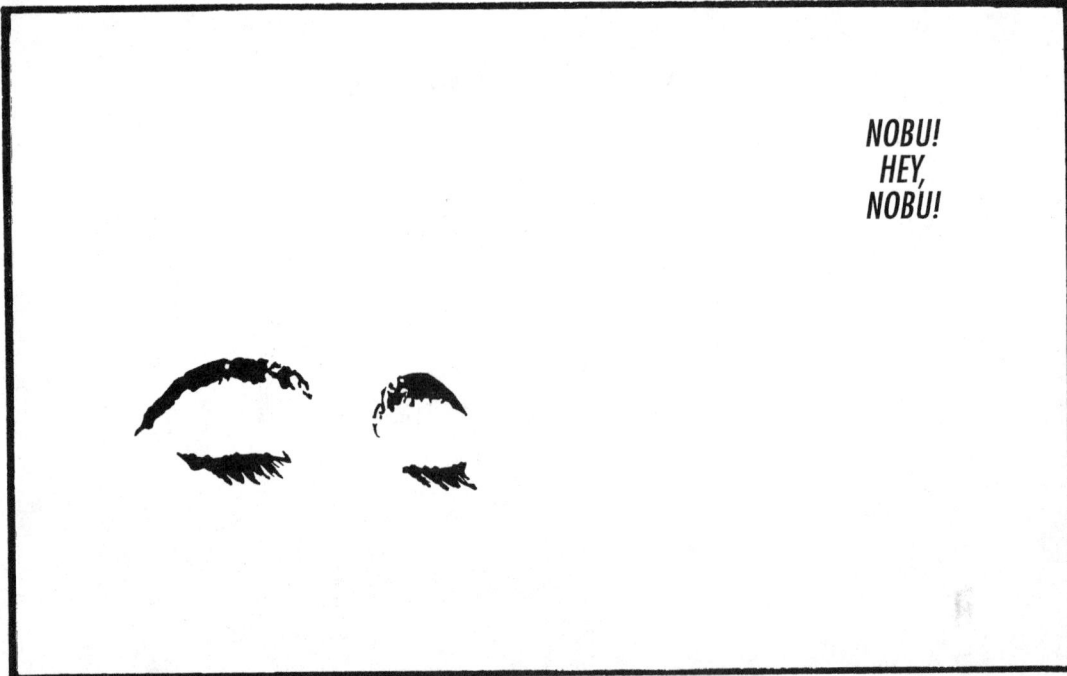

NOBU!
HEY,
NOBU!

TONIGHT'S
THE LAST
NIGHT.

HEY AYU!
WOULD IT BE
O.K. IF I LIVED
HERE?

57

RYOSUKE
BROUGHT
SOME CHICK
HOME, SO I
HAD TO GET
OUT OF
THERE. YOU
KNOW?

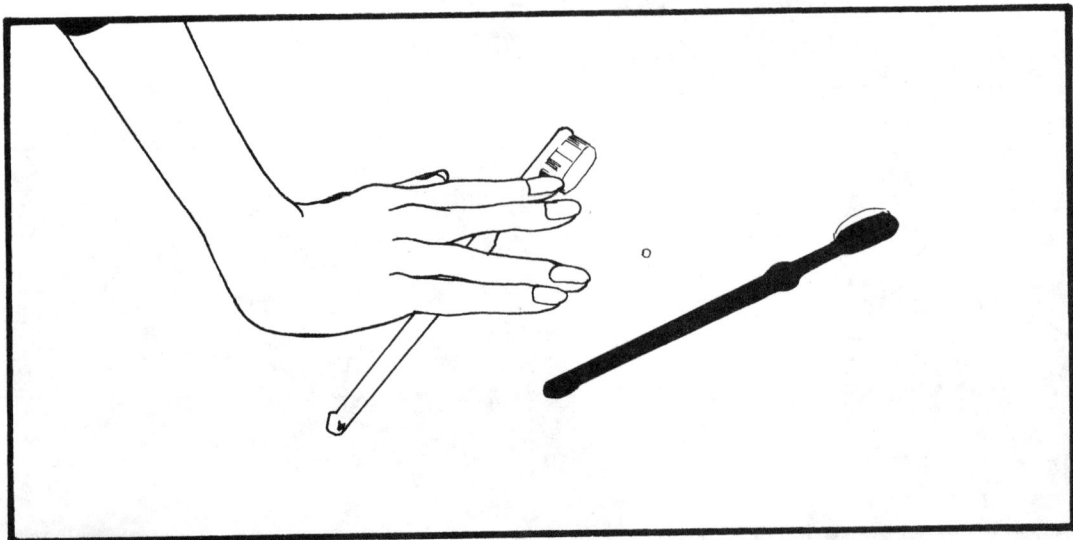

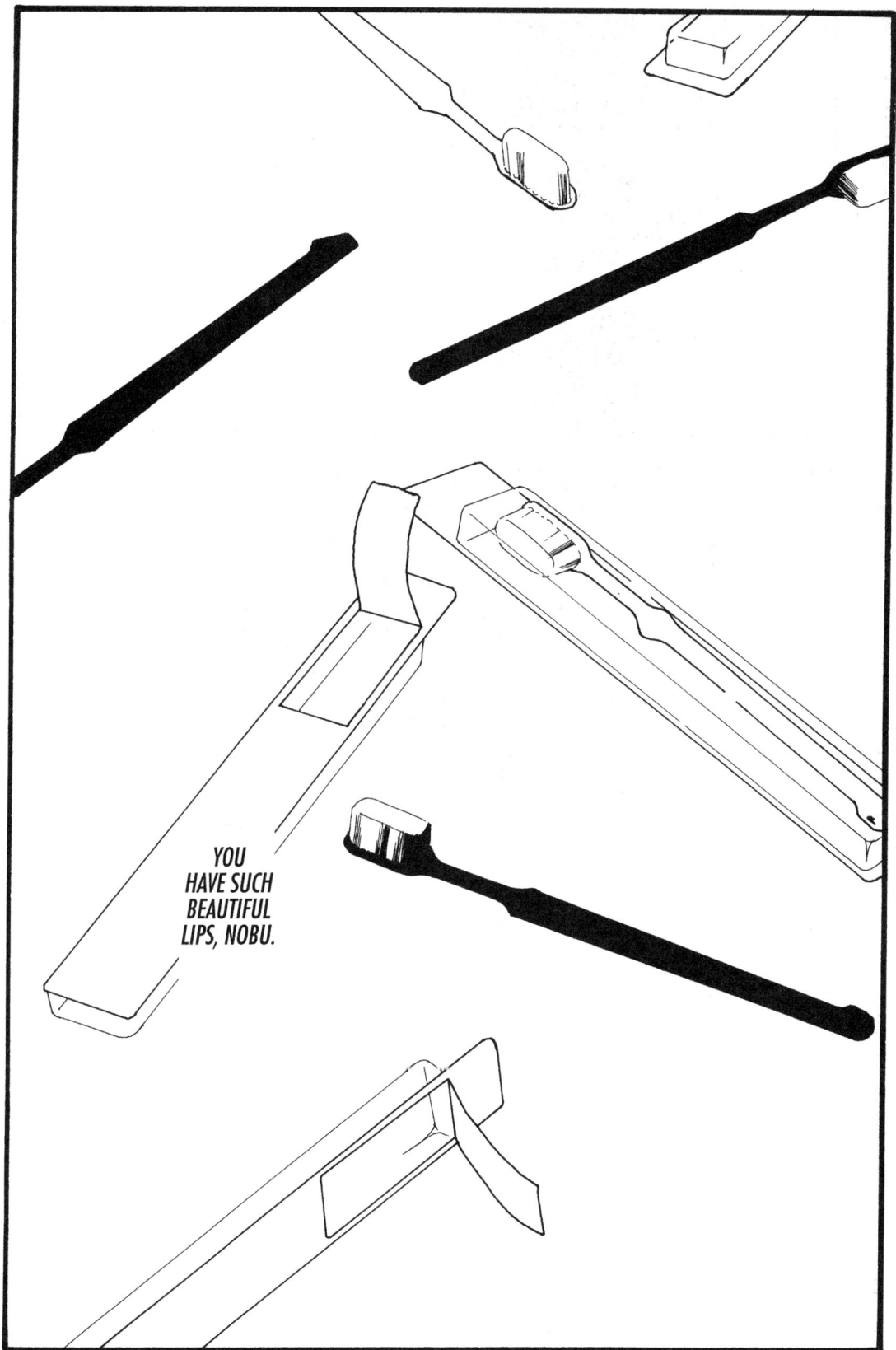

YOU HAVE SUCH BEAUTIFUL LIPS, NOBU.

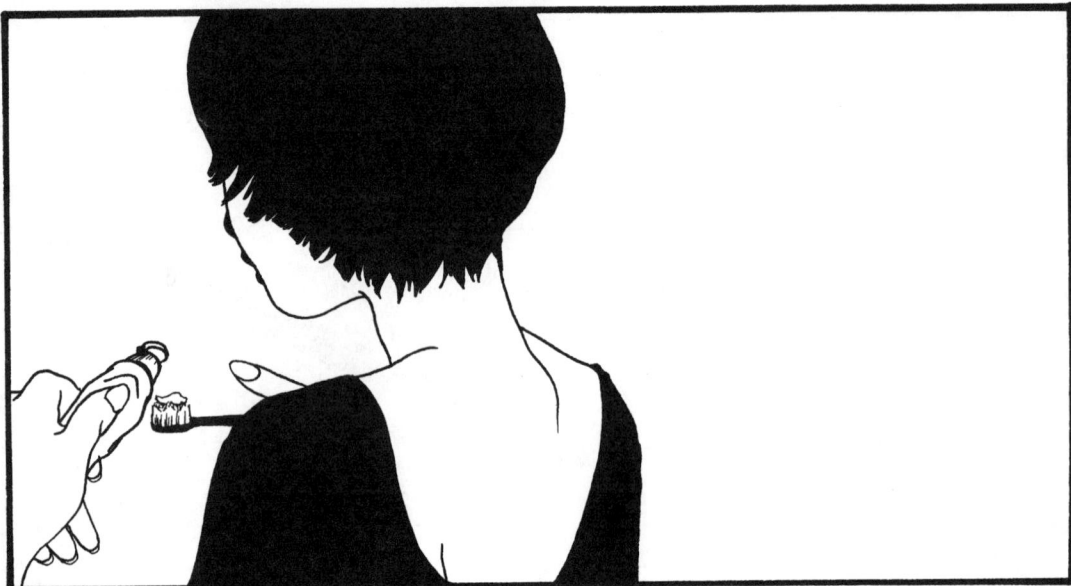

AYU, YOU SHOULD
NEVER FALL FOR
AN ASSHOLE
LIKE THAT. I
ALREADY MADE
THAT MISTAKE, O.K.?

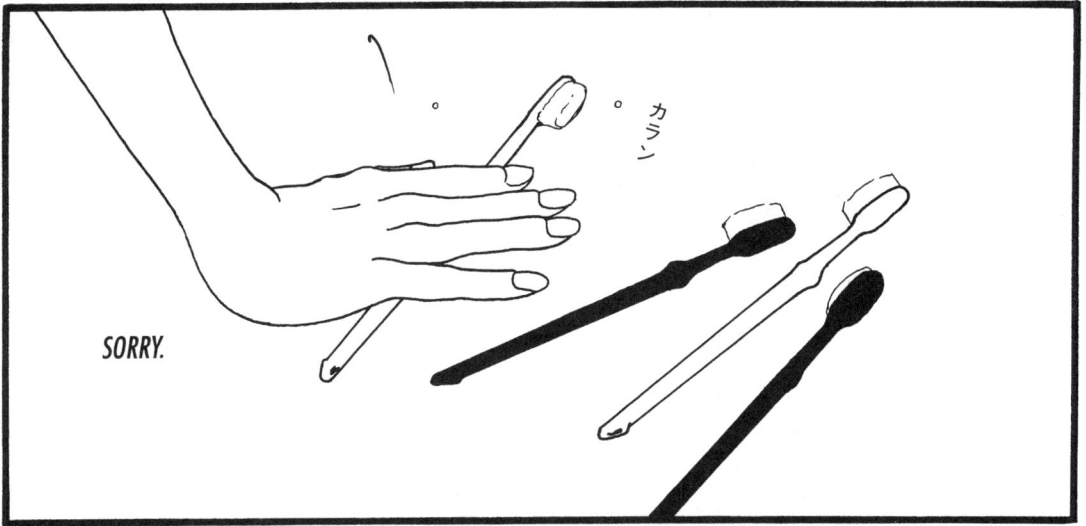

SORRY.

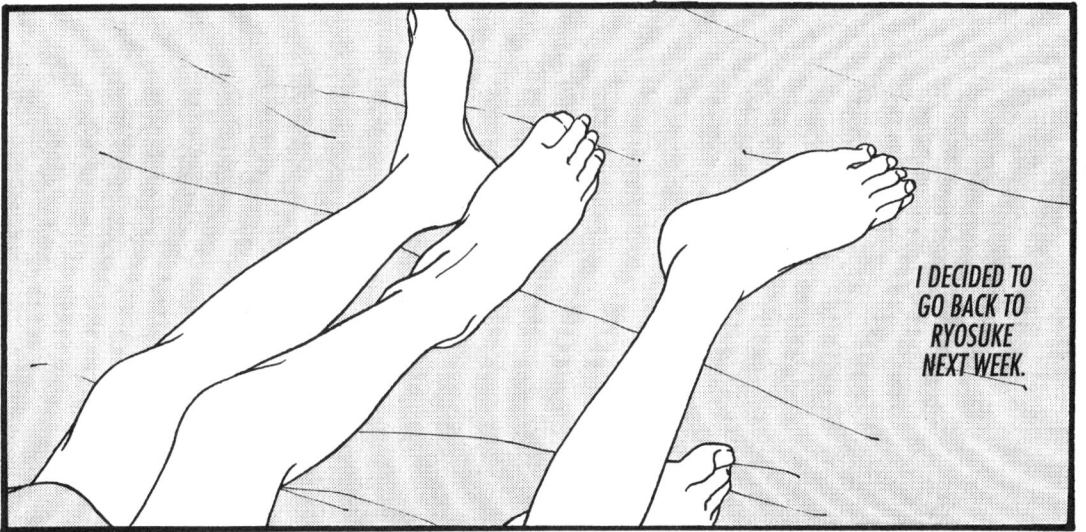

I DECIDED TO GO BACK TO RYOSUKE NEXT WEEK.

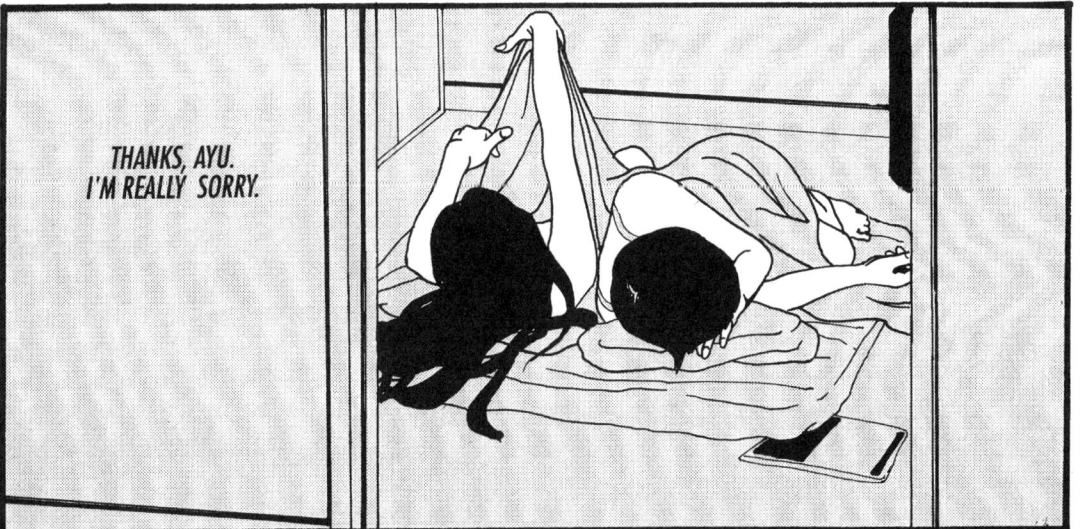

THANKS, AYU. I'M REALLY SORRY.

SO MANY TIMES. SO MANY TIMES I CAN'T EVEN
COUNT. THE PAIN IS INCREDIBLE. LIKE MORNING
SICKNESS, YET I VOMIT MOUTHFULS OF WHITE
BUBBLES AND BLOOD.

IT RUNS FROM THE MIDDLE OF MY
SPINE TO MY THROAT AND I CAN'T SEE
THROUGH IT TO FIND MY HEART.

DON'T GO.

IT'S KIND OF FUNNY, NOBU. YOU'LL USE MY GOOD-BYE GIFT WITHOUT EVEN KNOWING IT.

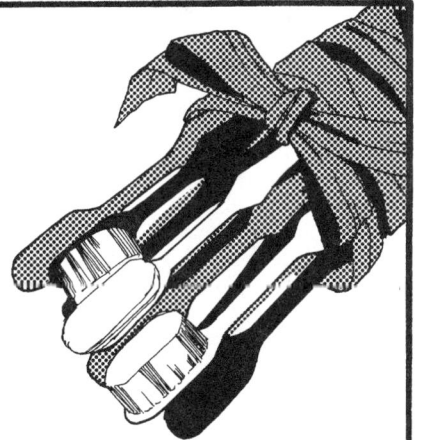

COMPLETELY UNAWARE AS
I COVER YOU IN KISSES.
... I LIKE THAT.

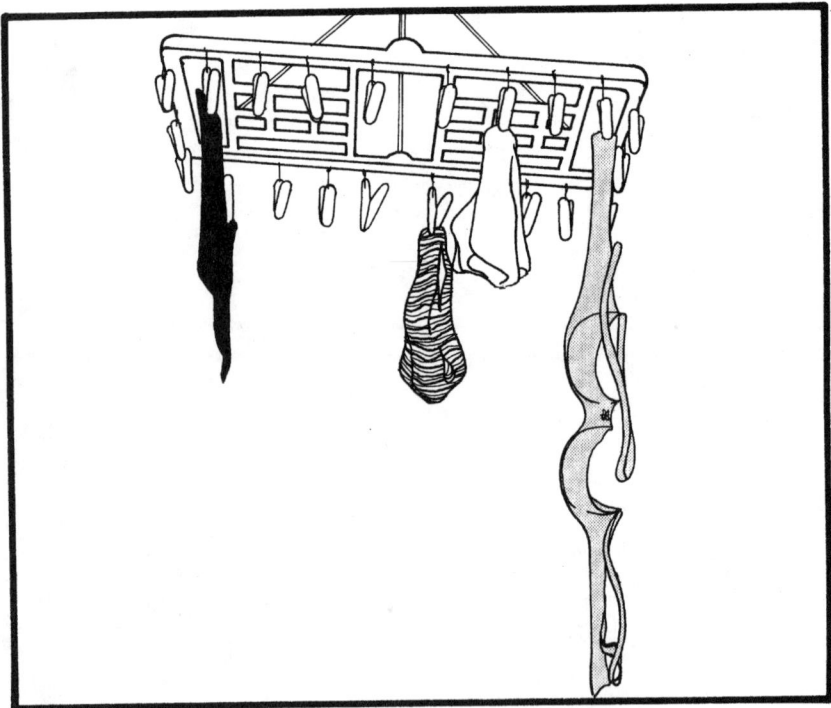

kitty court drama

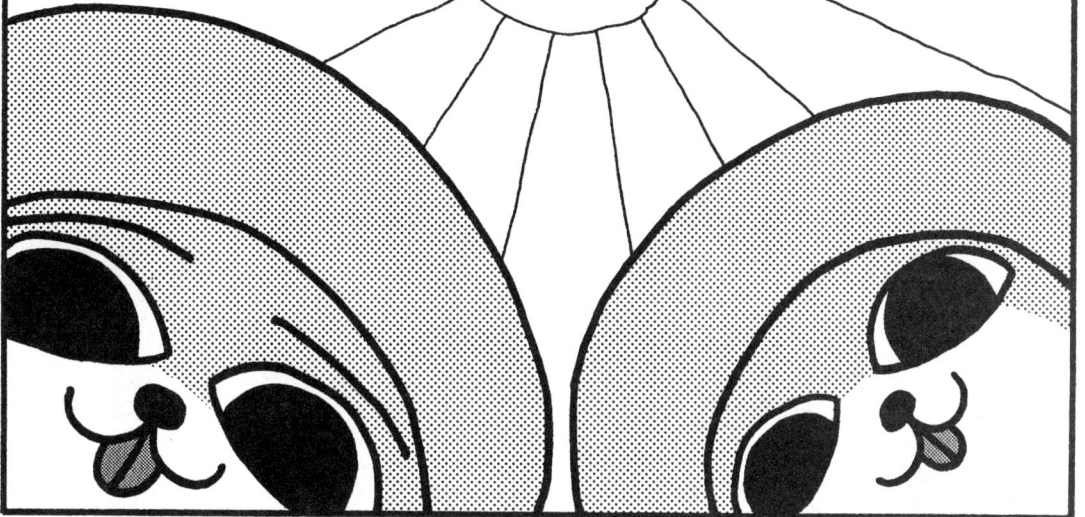

CRICKET FAMILY A-65, YOU ARE CHARGED WITH THE CRIME OF BEING INSECTS.

HOW DO YOU PLEAD?

YOUR HONOR, ALTHOUGH I MUST PLEAD GUILTY TO THESE CHARGES...

... I MUST STATE IN MY DEFENSE THAT I AM A HARD WORKING GROCER, AND FEEL THAT I HAVEN'T ACTUALLY BROKEN ANY LAWS.

COURT DISMISSED!

WHEW

YOU GUYS WAIT HERE! COURT'LL RESUME SAME TIME TOMORROW MORNING!

HOP

HOP

SPLASH!

ALL RIGHT! THEY'RE GONE!

HURRY UP, EVEYONE, LET'S GET OUT OF HERE!

B-BUT...

THE FROG TOLD US NOT TO GO ANYWHERE.

ARE YOU RETARDED OR WHAT?

YOU WANNA WAIT FOR THEM TO COME BACK SO THEY CAN GAS YOU TO DEATH?

70

THE END